A woman wearing a sky-blue jogging suit got into line behind me. She was holding a cereal box. She smiled at me, and I smiled back.

I decided to show her what a really good catcher I am. I made a wild and daring onion throw.

I missed the catch. The onion kept going, straight for the middle of the baby food castle. The castle was going to fall!

JULIAN'S WORLD

by Ann Cameron

JULIAN'S WORLD

GLORIA RISING

by Ann Cameron

illustrated by Lis Toft

A STEPPING STONE BOOK™
Random House New York

Text copyright © 2002 by Ann Cameron
Interior illustrations copyright © 2002 by Lis Toft
Cover illustration copyright © by Robert Papp

All rights reserved. Published in the United States by Random House Children's Books, a division of Penguin Random House LLC, New York. Originally published in hardcover by Farrar, Straus and Giroux LLC, New York, in 2002.

Random House and the colophon are registered trademarks and A Stepping Stone Book and the colophon are trademarks of Penguin Random House LLC.

This edition published by arrangement with Farrar, Straus and Giroux LLC, New York.

Visit us on the Web! rhcbooks.com

Educators and librarians, for a variety of teaching tools, visit us at RHTeachersLibrarians.com

Library of Congress Cataloging-in-Publication Data is available upon request.
ISBN 978-0-440-41998-3 (trade)

Printed in the United States of America
27 26 25 24 23 22 21 20 19 18

This book has been officially leveled by using the F&P Text Level Gradient™ Leveling System.

To Ryan; Riona; Courtland (III); Kevin, Jr.; Zachary;
Kristopher; Kemahni; and Courtney Boozé—
with admiration for their values and
great hopes for their futures
—A.C.

CONTENTS

The Astronaut and the Onion

My mother was making spaghetti sauce. She said, "Gloria, honey, would you go buy me an onion?"

"Sure," I said. She gave me some money, and I went.

The store was crowded with old people holding tightly to their shopping carts, little kids hollering to their parents for candy, and lots of people staring at shopping lists and blocking the aisles.

I ducked around all the carts and went to the back where the vegetables are. From all the onions in the bin, I took the prettiest—a big round one, light tan and shiny, with a silvery glow to its skin.

I carried it to the express checkout and stood at the end of a very long line.

Next to me there was a giant Berkbee's Baby Food display. It was like a wall of glass, and taller than I am. All the little jars were stacked up to look like a castle, with pennants that said "Baby Power" sticking out above the castle doorways and windows. At the top there was a high tower with a red-and-white flag that said "Berkbee's Builds Better Babies!" I started counting the jars, but when I got to 346, I gave up. There must have been at least a thousand.

The checkout line didn't move. To pass the time, I started tossing my onion from hand to hand. I tried to improve and make my throws harder to catch.

A woman wearing a sky-blue jogging suit got in line behind me. She was holding a cereal box. She smiled at me, and I smiled back.

I decided to show her what a really good catcher I am. I made a wild and daring onion throw.

I missed the catch. The onion kept going, straight for the middle of the baby food castle. The castle was going to fall!

My folks would have to pay for every broken jar! The store manager would kill me. After that, my folks would bring me back to life to tell me things that would be much worse than death.

I was paralyzed. I shut my eyes.

I didn't hear a crash. Maybe I had gone deaf from fright. Or maybe I was in a time warp because of my fear. In fifty years the onion

would land, and that would be the end of me.

I felt a tap on my shoulder. If I opened my eyes, I would see the store manager and all the broken jars.

I didn't want to see him. I didn't want to know how bad it was.

There came a tap again, right on the top of my head.

I heard a woman's voice. "I have your onion."

I opened my eyes. The woman in the jogging suit handed the onion to me.

"Lucky I used to play baseball," she said.

"O-o-o-h," I said. I clutched the onion.

"O-o-o-h," I moaned again.

"You're welcome," was all she said.

She had brown eyes with a sparkle in them, and her hair was in shiny black ringlets. She wore blue-green earrings that hung on tiny gold chains. When she tilted her head, her earrings spun around, and I saw they were the Earth—I mean, made to look like the Earth, jeweled with green continents and blue oceans.

"Your earrings are beautiful," I said.

She smiled. "Some friends got them for me," she said, "to remind me of a trip we made."

When she said "trip," her face started to look familiar, but I didn't know why. Then I remembered.

"I've seen you!" I said. "I saw you on TV!"

She smiled. "Could be."

"And you come from right here in town, but you don't live here anymore," I said.

"That's right," she said.

"And you are—aren't you?—Dr. Grace Street, the astronaut!"

She tilted her head, and the little Earths on both her ears spun round. "That's me," she said.

I was amazed, because I never thought I would meet a famous person in my life, and yet one was right beside me in the supermarket, and I myself, Gloria Jones, was talking to her, all because of my onion throw.

"We learned about the space station in school last year," I said. "You were up there, orbiting the Earth."

"My team and I were there," Dr. Street said.

"What is space like?"

"You know," she said.

"How could I know?" I said.

"We're always in space," Dr. Street said. "We're in space right now."

"Yes," I said, "but what was it like out there, where you went? Out there it must seem different."

"Do you really want to know?" she asked, and I said yes.

"The most awesome part was when we had to fix things on the outside of the station. We got our jobs done and floated in our space suits, staring out into the universe. There were zillions of stars—and space, deep and black, but it didn't seem exactly empty. It seemed to be calling to us, calling us to go on an endless journey. And that was very scary.

"So we turned and looked at Earth. We were two hundred miles above it. We saw enormous swirls of clouds and the glow of snowfields at the poles. We saw water like a giant blue cradle for the land. One big ocean, not 'oceans.' The Earth isn't really chopped up into countries, either. Up there you see it is one great big powerful living being that knows a lot, lot more than we do."

"What does it know?" I said.

"It knows how to be Earth," Dr. Street said. "And that's a lot."

I tried to imagine everything she had seen. It gave me a shiver.

"I wish I could see what you saw," I said. "I'd like to be an astronaut. Of course, probably I couldn't."

Dr. Street frowned. "Why do you say 'Probably I couldn't?' "

"Practically nobody gets to do that," I said.

"You might be one of the people who do," she said. "But you'll never do anything you want to do if you keep saying 'Probably I couldn't.' "

"But maybe I can't!" I protested. I looked down at my onion. I didn't think a very poor onion thrower had a chance to be an astronaut.

Dr. Street looked at my onion, too. "It was a good throw—just a bad catch," she said. "Anyhow—saying 'Maybe I can't' is different. It's okay. It's realistic.

"Even 'I can't' can be a good, sensible thing to say. It makes life simpler. When you really know you can't do one thing, that leaves you time to try some of the rest. But when you don't even know what you can do, telling yourself 'Probably I couldn't' will stop you before you even start. It's paralyzing. You don't want to be paralyzed, do you?"

"I just was paralyzed," I said. "A minute ago, when I threw my onion. I didn't enjoy it one bit."

"If you don't want to be paralyzed," Dr. Street said, "be careful what you tell yourself—because whatever you tell yourself you're very likely to believe."

I thought about what she said. "If maybe I could be an astronaut," I asked, "how would I get to be one?"

"You need to do well in school," she said. "And you need to tame your fears. Not get rid of them—just tame them."

The line moved forward suddenly, and we moved up. Maybe the people in line behind us thought Dr. Street and I were mother and daughter having a serious conversation, because they left some space around us.

"So how does a person tame fears?"

"By doing things that are difficult, and succeeding," Dr. Street said. "That's how you learn you can count on yourself. That's how you get confidence. But even then, you keep a little bit of fear inside—a fear that keeps you careful."

The checkout line moved again, and we moved with it.

"Big things are really little," Dr. Street said. "That's a great secret of life."

"How—" I began. But I never got to ask how big things are really little, because I was the first person in line.

The checkout man looked at my onion.

"Young lady, didn't you weigh that?" he asked.

"No, sir," I said.

"Go back to Produce and have it weighed."

So I had to go.

"Goodbye," Dr. Street said.

"Goodbye," I said. On the way to Produce, I looked back at her. She was walking toward the exit with her cereal box. I waved, but she didn't notice.

And I could see how little things are really big. Just on account of an onion, I had met an astronaut, and on account of that same onion, I had to stop talking to her.

But how big things are really little I couldn't understand at all.

My New Pet

The kitchen was full of pots and pans and steamy tomato smells. I set my onion down on a clear place on the table.

"At last!" my mom said. "What took so long?"

"There were a lot of people in the store, but guess what! Dr. Grace Street was there, and I talked to her!"

"Who?" my mom asked.

"Dr. Grace Street, the astronaut!" I said. "Don't you remember, we saw her on TV!"

My mom wiped her forehead with the back of her hand.

"There are so many famous people I can't keep track of them all," she said. "Was she the one who went up in the space shuttle?"

"She didn't just go up in the shuttle! She lived on the space station that's circling Earth. Mom, I talked to her! In the checkout line I played catch with the onion, and I missed, and Dr. Street caught it. That was how we met."

My mom picked up the onion and looked it over. "It seems fine."

She picked up a knife. She was going to peel the onion.

All of a sudden, I couldn't stand that.

"No! Please!" I reached out to protect it.

My mom stopped dead. "Gloria, for heaven's sake! I almost cut your hand!"

"Please, Mom!" I begged. "Don't peel it! Don't cut it!"

My mom stared at me. "Why not?"

"I want to keep it."

"Keep it!"

"It's kind of like an autographed baseball. An onion Dr. Street touched. Almost an autographed onion."

"Gloria, be reasonable! This is a nice big onion. Onions are to eat."

"Please, not this one," I said. "If you'll let me keep it, I'll get you another one. I'll go to the store right now!"

My mom sighed. She set the onion—my onion—in a bowl of fruit on the kitchen table.

"Be quick!" she said.

I got home again with an ordinary onion. My mom chopped it up, and I told her about Dr. Street.

She listened, but she had a hard "I am chopping" look on her face. As if she wasn't really impressed. As if all she could care about was spaghetti sauce.

I asked if she didn't think astronauts were important, and she said of course they were important.

I asked if she would want to be one.

She stopped chopping. "Definitely not," she said.

I couldn't believe it. "Even if you had the chance?"

"To me it would be like being stuck inside a tin can that a firecracker shoots into the air. And about that safe." She picked up her knife.

"But Dr. Street says it's beautiful!" I said. "It's beautiful to see the Earth from space."

"To me, the Earth is very beautiful seen from the Earth," my mom said. "I don't have to go someplace else to see it." She looked down at the cutting board and slapped bits of onion off her hands.

I felt as if I'd been to the moon and back but my mom didn't care.

"Oh," I said.

"You're disappointed in me, aren't you?" my mom said.

My hands squeezed together at my sides and my face felt pressed in.

"Yes."

"Gloria, I'm sorry," my mom said. "I know you just met someone special. I just haven't been where you've been. But I'm listening. I care."

"Really?" I said.

"Really!"

"Well then—I think I want to be an astronaut like Dr. Street and maybe a regular doctor, too. And you're probably going to tell me that I can't."

"No," my mom said, "I wouldn't tell you that. Those aren't the jobs for me. But if that's what's right for you, and you can do it, I'll be proud of you. And who knows, maybe you can."

I looked at the fruit bowl and my onion.

"Mom," I said, "may I keep this onion in my room?"

She thought, then shook her head. "It's better to keep it in the kitchen. If it's in your room, you will forget about it, and it will rot."

"But if it's in the kitchen, *you* will forget about it," I argued. "You will think it is any old onion, and you will chop it."

My mom hesitated.

"It's my only souvenir of meeting Dr. Street," I said. "I'll take care of it. I'll check it every day. If it rots, I'll throw it out."

"All right," she said. "I never heard of a girl with a pet onion, but if you want this one, it's yours."

She took it from the fruit bowl and handed it to me.

"I hope it brings you luck."

Me and the Dragon of Doom

My onion sat on my windowsill. The early morning sun shone in and made it glow just like a pearl. I admired it. Then I got ready for school.

I put on my brand-new shirt and my brand-new jeans, my brand-new shoes and my brand-new red headband with sparkles on it.

I got out my special brand-new blue erasers in the shape of teddy bears, and I stuck them on my two brand-new pencils. I hoped I'd do well in school, the way Dr. Street said. If I could go all year in fourth grade without one mistake, I would never have to mess up my teddy-bear erasers.

I put my brand-new notebooks and my brand-new pencils with the teddy-bear erasers in my brand-new backpack. I went to say good-bye to my onion.

It was looking more beautiful than ever—too beautiful to leave behind. I slipped it into my backpack.

Going out the door, I popped a big pink square of bubble gum into my mouth. It came wrapped in a little comic strip, which I saved in my pocket.

That pink gum is tough, kind of like chewing a brick, but soon I got it softened up. I made enormous pink bubbles all the way to school.

It's hard when you're by yourself to know exactly how big a bubble-gum bubble you've made. That's one reason it's good to have friends.

There were a lot of kids on the steps of school. I thought I saw my friend Julian coming up the walk. I blew my last bubble even bigger, just for him.

Unfortunately, he stopped to talk to his brother, Huey. He didn't see me.

Unfortunately, the bubble burst and spattered, practically on the face of the person right behind me.

Unfortunately, the person right behind me was Mrs. Priscilla Yardley. Mrs. Yardley was going to be my fourth-grade teacher. Mrs. Yardley is the teacher kids call "the Dragon of Doom."

She glared at me, but before she could say anything, a boy named Billy Watkins held the door open for her, and she hoisted her big black briefcase higher and walked in.

"Thank you! What a young gentleman!" she

said to Billy. She smiled, and she forgot all about me.

When she smiled, she didn't have such a bad face. She couldn't help it that her lips were so flat they looked like a piece of a measuring tape—the metal kind carpenters use that stretches and then snaps shut with a click.

Mrs. Yardley walked in front of me down the hall. Mr. Dixon, the principal, has a glass wall outside his office, and she stopped there to look at her reflection. She gave herself a hard look, up and down, as if she wasn't going to be fooled, even by herself. Then she straightened her black-and-white-striped jacket and smiled a little smile at herself—as if there had been a difficult test and she had passed it.

I walked by Mrs. Yardley, and then I saw my last year's teacher, Ms. Morgan. She is my most favorite teacher I have ever had. When I said hi to her, she put down all the stuff she was carrying and gave me a hug.

Mrs. Yardley went by, looked at us, and frowned.

"What's new?" Ms. Morgan asked.

"I have beautiful erasers for starting school," I said. "Also, I have an onion that an astronaut held. You can touch it!"

I opened my backpack. Ms. Morgan reached a finger in and touched my onion. "Neat," she said.

I went on down the hall and turned into the fourth-grade room. A lot of kids were already sitting down. There were name tags on all the desks. My friends Julian and Latisha were sitting down at the back of the room. My desk was halfway to the front, right ahead of Billy Watkins's. I sat down and stored my notebooks, my pencils, and my onion.

Mrs. Yardley wrote her name on the board in nice even letters. She took the yardstick by the blackboard and underlined her name twice.

"See how evenly I write," she said. "You can

learn to do that, too. And this is how you spell my name," she added. "Don't forget the 'd.' On every paper, I want you to write 'Mrs. Yardley's Class' in the left-hand top corner, and your own name in the top right corner. Very neatly, please!"

She tapped her yardstick against the blackboard twice, and looked at us hard to make sure we were all paying attention.

"Maybe you have heard that I am the strictest teacher in the school. It is true.

"I am not a huggy teacher. We are going to work hard this year. We are not going to have hamsters, turtles, or algae in jars. We are going to have flash cards. We're going to use them a lot to get ready for some very important state tests."

The whole class groaned. It used to be okay to groan in Ms. Morgan's class.

"No groans!" Mrs. Yardley commanded. "Also, I don't permit gum-chewing in my class. Do you have gum in *your* mouth, Gloria Jones?"

I wasn't even chewing it, I had stored it behind my back molars.

"Yes, Mrs. Yardley," I said.

"Take it out!" Mrs. Yardley commanded, pointing at me with her yardstick.

"Yes, Mrs. Yardley," I said. I took the gum out of my mouth. She never said to put it in the wastebasket, so I just rolled it in a ball and wrapped it in its comic strip wrapper and put it in my desk. It was still good. I didn't want to waste it.

We did vocabulary flash cards, and then we did math review. After recess, when we came in for silent reading, Mrs. Yardley looked happier. She had the yardstick by her side. She was sitting at her desk with a thick book called *Respecting the Rules* and a big cup of black coffee.

We picked up our books, and Mrs. Yardley

picked up hers. I read mine some, but I kept watching Mrs. Yardley. She turned a few pages of *Respecting the Rules* and smiled. She spooned sugar into her coffee and stirred it. And then, all of a sudden, she roared and hissed—just like a dragon. Just like the Dragon of Doom.

"Thisss iss the mosst dissgussting thing I have ever ssseen!"

Nobody knew what she was talking about, but everybody ducked low—me most of all, because Mrs. Yardley jumped out of her chair with her coffee cup and her spoon and she came straight at me.

"Gloria Jones, do you recognize thisss?" she said. She dipped her spoon deep into her coffee and held up what was down there.

It was like a great swamp monster. It was soppy and drippy and had colored paper stuck around it. Underneath the paper and the brown juice of the coffee, I could see pink.

"It looks like bubble gum," I said. "But it's not my gum. My gum is right here in my desk!"

I opened my desk to show her. Mrs. Yardley peered in.

"Where?" she demanded.

I couldn't find my gum. It was gone.

I pointed to Mrs. Yardley's spoon. "Maybe that is my gum," I said, "but I didn't put it in your coffee! Honest!"

I couldn't tell if she believed me. She didn't say. She went over to the wastebasket and dumped the gum and the wrapper into it. It was still good gum when I saved it. Now I was never even going to get to read the comic it was wrapped in. I should've read it in the first place.

Out in the hall, Mrs. Yardley dumped her coffee in the water fountain.

When she came back in, I raised my hand. "Mrs. Yardley, why—"

What I meant to ask her was, why adults think things are disgusting that kids don't think are disgusting. Like bubble gum. Did Mrs. Yardley like bubble gum when she was a kid? Was there one particular day when she grew up and all of a sudden it looked disgusting to her? And if so, why?

But I didn't get a chance to ask.

Mrs. Yardley picked up her yardstick. She pointed it at me. "No questions from you! Let me see your desk! Open it!"

She leaned over me with the perfumy sleeve of her black-and-white jacket in my face.

I creaked my desktop up.

"That!" she said, pointing at my onion with her yardstick. "What is it?"

"It's an onion," I said.

Anybody could see it was an onion. Especially Mrs. Yardley. I could already tell she had very good eyes.

"You brought an *onion* to school? May I ask *what* you are planning to do with it?"

"It's just here, with me," I said. "A famous astronaut who went up in space caught it. So that's why I have it."

"I never heard such bubble-babble in my life!" Mrs. Yardley said. "Put that onion in your backpack! Take it home today! If I ever see an onion here again, it's going in the trash!"

Julian raised his hand.

"Yes, Julian," Mrs. Yardley said.

"An astronaut really did catch it, Mrs. Yardley," Julian said. "Gloria told me."

"I don't care who caught it," Mrs. Yardley said. "In this classroom there will be no hamsters, no turtles, no algae, no gum, and no onions."

She went back to the front of the room and put her yardstick down against the blackboard.

"Class, face forward and sit up straight! Return to your silent reading. And you, Gloria, will be staying after school."

I never had to stay after school before. I didn't know what it would be like.

Mrs. Yardley told me what she wanted me to do. Write fifty times "I will not be disrespectful in class again." And number my sentences.

Then she went out of the room and left me to do it.

I got out my notebook paper, but I couldn't write what she said. Because I hadn't been disrespectful, so I couldn't say I wouldn't do it *again*. I wrote everything she had told me except the "again," fifty times.

Then I waited for her to come back and ask me why I had left out a word.

After a while she did come back. I held out my two sheets of paper from my almost brand-new notebook.

She counted up all my sentences. When she saw I had done fifty, she gave me a little measuring-tape smile. She never even noticed that I didn't write "again."

"Have you learned your lesson, Gloria?" she asked.

I didn't say anything.

I thought of pointing out that I hadn't written "again" and telling her why, but I didn't.

Maybe I was learning my lesson.

Ms. Morgan

The corridor felt cold and empty. All the class-room doors were closed. Then I came to Ms. Morgan's, and it was open. She was pinning pinecones and leaves and paper butterflies on the third-grade bulletin board.

"Hi!" I said. I felt shy.

"Gloria!" Ms. Morgan said. "What are you doing here so late?"

"Going home," I said.

"I want to get home, too," she said. "But since you're still here, could you help me for a minute?" She handed me a pinecone, and I pinned it on the board. She pinned a butterfly on my pinecone.

We pinned up a lot of them like that, and then Ms. Morgan dropped some food pellets into Willy the hamster's cage.

"Finished!" she said. "I had a long day."

"Me too," I said. My voice kind of trembled when I said it.

"With Mrs. Yardley?" Ms. Morgan asked.

"Yes. She made me stay after school. I never ever had to do that before."

"Why did she keep you after?" Ms. Morgan asked.

I told her everything, and how I couldn't write what Mrs. Yardley told me to write.

"What did Mrs. Yardley say?" Ms. Morgan asked.

"She took my writing and she didn't even notice," I said.

"That's probably all to the good," Ms. Mor-

gan said. "Mrs. Yardley likes things exactly her way."

"She says she doesn't like turtles, hamsters, or hugging. She doesn't like bubble gum, either. I think she hates it. And I don't think she is ever going to like me."

"She has some prejudices," Ms. Morgan said. "As we all do. And once she thinks she's measured a person, it's hard for her to change her mind. But you just do your best, Gloria, and I think she'll see she's measured you wrong."

"I don't care what she sees," I said.

Ms. Morgan dropped a few extra pellets of food into Willy's cage.

"You probably do care, though, down deep," Ms. Morgan said.

"You know what?" I said. "I wish I had failed last year. Then I could still be in your class."

"That would have been terrible!" Ms. Morgan said. "You are a good student, Gloria. You need new times, new things to learn, and new things to happen. Mrs. Yardley isn't the easiest person to get along with, but she knows a lot."

"I like the old times," I said. "I like Willy." I stuck my finger into his cage. He jumped off his wheel, and he wiggled his little nose all over my finger.

"You and Willy are still friends," Ms. Morgan said. "You and I are still friends."

Ms. Morgan got her jacket and her purse. She started to turn out the lights, and then she paused with her hand on the switch.

"Shall I tell you something?" she said.

"What?"

"I don't know if it was the right thing to do, or if it was wise—but I understand why you didn't write what Mrs. Yardley told you. And I think you were brave."

The Forest of Pencils

Back when I was in Ms. Morgan's class there were lots of good times, all different. In Mrs. Yardley's class, the only good time was Grinding Time.

Grinding Time was when we all sharpened our pencils.

Our room had two pencil sharpeners, but Mrs. Yardley didn't want us using them whenever we felt like it. She had picked the time right before afternoon recess for us to sharpen our pencils.

We went up to the pencil sharpeners by twos and sharpened as hard as we could. My friend Latisha tried to get a rhythm into the grinding, and Shavaun tried to grind his louder than the kid at the other sharpener. The noise was tremendous.

Julian doesn't like noise that much. He liked to be the one to find out a sharpener was full of wood shavings and ask if he could dump them in the trash. He didn't spill them on the floor on purpose like some other kids, so Mrs. Yardley would let him do it. Usually it was hard to get the pencil sharpener back together again. Sometimes Mrs. Yardley would let two or three kids get up to put it back together, because she wasn't good at it herself. And she'd say thank you.

This particular day seemed like all the others. We got through to Grinding Time, we had our pencils sharpened, we held them up so Mrs. Yardley could see the points, and then we went to recess.

Over by the swings, Billy Watkins called Julian a sissy.

"Me? A sissy?" Julian said. He was more surprised than mad.

"If you weren't a sissy," Billy said, "you'd dump pencil shavings on the floor. The only reason you don't is that you're scared of the Dragon."

"I'm not scared of anybody!" Julian said.

"You're scared of Mrs. Yardley. Onion Head is scared of her, too!"

Billy always called me "Onion Head" since he saw my onion in my desk the first day of school. I was glad I had it back home on my windowsill where it was safe.

"My name is not Onion Head, and I am not scared!" I said.

"You make me sick, Onion Head. I have to go barf," Billy said. And he ran into school with his hand over his mouth. So there wasn't any fight, because you can't fight with somebody who ran away to vomit.

The bell rang. We walked back into class. Mrs. Yardley glared at us as we walked in. She was holding on to her yardstick so hard her knuckles were white.

We wondered what was the matter, and we sat down at our desks, very quiet.

"Who did this? That's what I want to know!" Mrs. Yardley said.

"Did what?" Julian asked.

Mrs. Yardley motioned at the ceiling with her yardstick. "You know! Look up, all of you! Look up!"

We looked up.

"Wow!" Ashok Seng said softly. He turned around and whispered to me, "It looks like a forest!"

Dozens and dozens of pencils were stuck in the white acoustic tiles of the ceiling.

"Open your desks! Show me your pencils!" Mrs. Yardley demanded.

All our desktops rose. I looked for my pencils, but I couldn't find them—my favorite ones with the blue teddy-bear erasers. And then on the ceiling I saw the little teddy bears looking at me sadly, with their smiles upside down. Right between them was the eraser-less tip of Mrs. Yardley's red correction pencil.

Mrs. Yardley came over to my desk with her yardstick. She peered down into my face.

"Isn't that my pencil between yours—the ones with the teddy-bear erasers?" she asked.

"Yes, Mrs. Yardley, it is. But I—"

Behind me, Billy Watkins lowered his desktop and raised his hand. His two green pencils stuck out like extra fingers.

"I have my pencils right here, Mrs. Yardley," he said. "Everybody else did it, but I didn't! They couldn't make me!" He looked at her, just waiting to be believed.

"We didn't stick our pencils up there!" Latisha said.

"No, we didn't," everybody protested. But Mrs. Yardley didn't listen.

"I'm sure you didn't do this, Billy," she said. "The rest of you, since you can't do your writing assignment, will get F's for the afternoon, and a note to your parents on your report cards."

She sent Billy to get Mr. Bullock, the janitor.

Mr. Bullock came back with Billy and looked up at the ceiling and shook his head and sighed. He left, and returned with a very tall ladder.

"Mr. Bullock, I'm going to discuss this with Mr. Dixon," Mrs. Yardley said. "Don't you talk, and don't you bother Mr. Bullock one bit!" she said to us. And she left.

Mr. Bullock spread out the legs of the ladder, and we moved our desks so he could get to all the pencils. Every time he went up and down, he came back with four or five pencils, and he held them out so the kids who owned them could come get them. Then he would move the ladder, go back up, groan a little bit, because he has arthritis, and reach for pencils again.

Finally he had them all. He put Mrs. Yardley's red correction pencil on her desk.

"Did you kids really do this?" he asked.

"No," we said. "We didn't do it."

"I didn't think so," Mr. Bullock said. "I know a lot of you are pretty good kids and would have more consideration for me."

That night, Julian, Latisha, Huey, and I talked about Mrs. Yardley and the forest of pencils. We'd made a spaceship in Julian and Huey's tree house, so we went up there after dark to talk about it. The spaceship is really good. It has dials and steering stuff and lights.

We pretended to steer it high above the

Earth, where the extra radiation might help us think. We talked about what our parents had told us—and all our parents said the same. They said we'd just have to bear with Mrs. Yardley, because sometimes life is like that. They said if we behaved the way we should, one day the truth would come out about who did it. Sometimes things work out by themselves, they said. And sometimes things don't work out at all, so you just try to keep cheerful and go on to the next thing.

We hoped the radiation was going to help us figure out who put the pencils in the ceiling. We figured it had to be somebody who didn't like Mrs. Yardley or anybody in our class.

We figured the person just about had to be Billy Watkins.

The next day we found out most of the kids in our class thought the same. But nobody, with or without radiation, could think of what to do about it.

Two Jobs

"Learning about careers will help you mature," Mrs. Yardley said. So we had to study up on a job and talk about it. It was my turn and Billy's turn the same day.

Mrs. Yardley called on Billy first. He went up to the front of the room, carrying a rolled-up paper.

"Today, I'm going to tell you about being a diplomat," Billy said. "It's what I want to be when I grow up. You probably don't know what a diplomat is. Diplomats are people who speak for their country when it talks to another country about problems. Sometimes diplomats help make treaties. Treaties are promises countries make to each other about what they will do or not do.

"Being a diplomat is a very important job. It's almost like being a spy. Sometimes a diplomat tells the truth, and sometimes not. Sometimes a diplomat is supposed to fool diplomats from other countries."

Latisha raised her hand. "But if they found out they were fooled, it could make them mad. It could start a war."

Mrs. Yardley said, "I don't think telling lies is an important part of the job, Billy. Making peace is. But go on . . ."

Billy unrolled the paper in his hand and showed it to us. "This here is a photo of my grandfather," Billy said. And he unrolled the photo and showed it to us. The photo was of an older man standing by some flowers in a yard.

"My grandfather is a diplomat and ambassador to the Antarctic—the South Pole," Billy said.

"But almost nobody lives on the South Pole!" Betty Roberts said. "Just a few people who do research on ice live there! And it's not a country. So no ambassador would be there."

"I don't know why, but my grandpa is ambassador there anyway," Billy said. "He told me he was going to come and see me for my birthday, but that was a lie, because he didn't come. That's how I know diplomats lie. And my parents are diplomats also. They told me they weren't going to divorce, but now they are."

Mrs. Yardley frowned. "Billy," she said, "what you're saying doesn't have to do with your topic. It's neither here nor there."

Julian raised his hand. "It's not here, and it's not there, but it's somewhere," he said.

"Saying something is neither here nor there

means it's off the subject," Mrs. Yardley explained. "It's not relevant. R-e-l-e-v-a-n-t." Mrs. Yardley spelled it out. "That's a word I want you all to look up for tomorrow."

Julian raised his hand. "But still, when something is neither here nor there, it can still be inside you where you think about it. And that is somewhere."

"That's enough, Julian," Mrs. Yardley warned. "You are not being relevant, either. Billy, is your talk concluded?"

"I guess so," Billy said. He rolled up the photo of his grandfather.

"Thank you, Billy. Your report was very interesting," Mrs. Yardley said. "And now we'll hear from Gloria."

I went up to the front. I looked around at everybody. They all look different and a little scary when you are the only one at the front of the room. When I swallowed, I felt as if my throat was rolling in reverse.

I took a deep breath. "I'm going to tell you about being an astronaut, which is what I'd like to be.

"To be an astronaut, you have to study a lot and tame your fears. If you go up in a spaceship, you live like on Earth, but very differently, too. A long way from Earth, there is almost no gravity.

"The fun part is sleeping, because you can just sleep in the air without a bed, and float around all night in your sleep. But if you don't want to wake up bumping into the ceiling, you wear a special belt that holds you to your bed.

"The bad part is, when you eat, you have to suck all your food, mushed up like baby food, out of a straw or a tube. If you put the food on a plate, it would just float around. Before you could catch it, food would get in the machinery and break it. Or you might end up breathing it and choke.

"I know some of this because I actually met

an astronaut this summer. Her name is Dr. Grace Street, and she's from here. She caught my onion in the supermarket—"

"Was it running away?" Billy said, and everybody laughed, even Mrs. Yardley.

"No, I threw it and she caught it. And you should have more respect for me—you shouldn't call me Onion Head!"

"No arguments during speeches," Mrs. Yardley said. "This is neither here nor there. Continue, Gloria."

"I'm done," I said.

"You gave a good report," Mrs. Yardley said, "but I don't see how you could have met Dr. Street in the supermarket this summer. I read in the paper that she was training in Russia then. I don't see how she would have been here, in the supermarket."

"I guess she wanted cereal," I said.

Everybody laughed. I tried to look like I thought it was funny, too.

"I mean, she was buying cereal. I don't know why she was here, she just was. And she said maybe I could be an astronaut like her."

Mrs. Yardley smiled her tiniest tape-measure smile—about a sixteenth of an inch. "I think you have a very vivid imagination, Gloria. As I said, your report was good—but you need to get control of that imagination. With an imagination like that, you probably couldn't be an astronaut."

"It's not imagination. I met her!" I said.

Mrs. Yardley smiled. "I'll tell you what, Gloria. Bring us a letter from Dr. Street confirming the fact that she met you. We would all like to see it."

A Letter

My parents didn't like it that Mrs. Yardley didn't believe me. They said that when they had a parent-teacher conference, they would talk to her about it.

They thought I should write a letter to Dr. Street, and ask her to write back.

They said a letter would probably reach her eventually if I sent it care of the President. I should put my address and my phone number in the letter, too—just in case she called.

Dr. Grace Street
Care of the President
The White House
Washington, D.C.

Dear Dr. Street,
              Remember me? You caught
my onion in the supermarket last summer.
(Thank you again!) You inspired me. I still
have the onion, it is on my windowsill.
    I have a problem. I told my teacher
and my class that I met you, and they
don't believe me. Especially my teacher
doesn't. My teacher said she would
believe me if I showed her a letter from
you.
    Right now, she thinks our class is bad,
and that I'm the worst. That's because
a boy named Billy stuck all our pencils
in the ceiling and blamed it on us.
    I know you are busy, but please,
please write me back. Unless you never
met me, and the woman in the supermarket
that I met was an Astronaut Impostor.
That would be the worst.
    Please tell me you are real.

                         Sincerely yours,
                         Gloria Jones

The Guest

No letter came from Dr. Street. Fall came, and it got colder outside. At school, Mrs. Yardley held on to her yardstick a lot more, as if it would keep her warm.

Sometimes she used it for drawing on the blackboard, but sometimes she pounded it next to our feet. Some kids said that when she was first named the Dragon of Doom, she used to hit students with it—back in the time before that was against the law.

This particular day, she tapped it three times against the blackboard.

"Class, our school is having a guest today. I told Mr. Dixon that this class, of all classes, doesn't *deserve* a guest, but he said the guest is an old friend of his and it's a special opportunity, so we are getting a guest anyway. I hope you will be courteous."

While she was saying this, I could see the shadow of someone standing outside the door. And then the person came in. She was smiling, just like we weren't the worst class in the world. Her hair was in black ringlets. She was wearing a red dress with suns on it, gold shoes, and earrings in the shape of planet Earth that turned round and round. And I knew her.

She and Mrs. Yardley shook hands, and Mrs. Yardley smiled a very wide measuring-tape smile—about two inches. Mrs. Yardley said, "It's an honor." Then she turned to us and said, "I want you all to be one hundred percent attentive to our guest, the astronaut Dr. Grace Street!"

Everybody clapped. I clapped extra hard and hoped that Dr. Street would see me, but it seemed as if she didn't, she just smiled at all of us.

She started talking. She told us how it was to orbit the Earth, and how she wanted to go back, and how she got to go there. The essential thing, she said, was that she had learned to tame her fears.

"That's the main thing I hope you will remember from today. Your life can be wonderful if you dare to face your fears.

"See, all of us human beings are full of energy. If our eyes were so good that we could see our own atoms, we'd actually see our energy like a great big whirling fireball inside us.

"However, sometimes we put a lot of that energy into fear. We get so afraid of failing we don't even dare think about what we'd like to be and do. Then we turn our energy into a great big swirling gray fearball that paralyzes us. But if we dare to challenge that fearball, we can find the fireball inside it, with all our hopes and dreams.

"Do you know what I mean?"

"I don't get it at all," Betty said.

Shavaun raised his hand. "Is a fearball like when you want to make a friend, but you get afraid maybe you can't? Or you want to try out for a team, but you're afraid of how you'll feel if you don't get chosen, so you don't try out?"

Dr. Street nodded. Her Earth earrings spun around. "That's it exactly!" she said. "We get a fearball when we think so much about everything bad that could happen that we forget good things can happen, too. The fearball grows because we forget that failure is just a part of life we can learn from."

Julian raised his hand. "So if our eyes can't

see them," Julian said, "how do we find a fearball or a fireball?"

"Try to do something you care about that
you're afraid you can't do," Dr. Street said.
"Then you'll feel a fearball and a fireball, and
you'll know what I mean. Any more questions?"

Kids started asking questions. Lots of them.
I wanted to ask one, too. I wanted to ask, "Do
you know me?" But every time I tried to raise
my hand, I felt a big swirling fearball inside
me, pulling my hand down. If I asked my ques-
tion and Dr. Street didn't know me, I didn't
think I could stand it.

I pushed my arm and I pushed on it more,
but I couldn't get my hand any higher than my
ear. My fearball wouldn't let me.

"No more questions?" Dr. Street said, and
the room was quiet. Soon Dr. Street would go.
I hadn't dared to challenge my fearball at all.

Mrs. Yardley touched Dr. Street's arm.

"Dr. Street," she said, "I want to introduce one special student, Gloria Jones. She made a class report on the career of being an astronaut. Would you stand up, Gloria, and say hello to a real astronaut?"

I was shocked. I knew Mrs. Yardley didn't think that I was special. She was asking me to stand up so when Dr. Street didn't recognize me, the whole class would know I had told a lie.

I stood up. Dr. Street looked at me. She had a little smile on her face, but I couldn't see any recognition in her eyes. Probably she met about a zillion new people a week, and probably she had never got my letter, either.

"Speak, Gloria!" Mrs. Yardley commanded.

"Hello, Dr. Street," I said. "Do you remember me? Me, from the supermarket?"

And Dr. Street said, "Gloria, of course I do! Thank you for your letter. The White House forwarded it to me. How are you, and how is your onion?"

A great wave of fear went out of me. A great warm wave of something good came in.

"My onion is fine," I said. "It is holding up just great."

"Come up here," Dr. Street said, so I went up to the front of the room. Dr. Street asked me to stand between her and Mrs. Yardley, and then Dr. Street shook my hand.

"You probably don't know this, Mrs. Yardley, but I have met Gloria before. In the supermarket, I caught an onion she threw. And I was very impressed with her because of the good questions she asked me. She is the kind of student who could be an astronaut one day."

"Oh, she couldn't," Mrs. Yardley said.

I guess nobody ever disagreed with Dr. Grace Street very much. She looked surprised. She stared at Mrs. Yardley.

"Mrs. Yardley, with all due respect, I think I'm a better judge of what it takes to be an astronaut than you are."

I had never heard anybody disagree with Mrs. Yardley to her face before. Maybe Mrs. Yardley had never had it happen, either. All the straight lines in her face cracked up like broken eggshell, and her ruler lips looked as if they'd split.

"It's not only Gloria," Mrs. Yardley said huffily. "I'm afraid this entire class is not high-achieving."

"But it could be," Dr. Street said. She looked at us. "I hope you'll work and use all your intelligence. Don't give up a single bit of it because somebody else thinks you're not smart.

"To get to be an astronaut, first I had to learn the things you're learning now. I learned to pass vocabulary tests and give answers to flash cards and all that. I know you can do it, too.

Surprise Mrs. Yardley! Show her you can do it! Can you?"

"Yes!" we said.

"Will you?" she asked.

We said yes again, with a lot of enthusiasm. Mrs. Yardley looked as if she would faint.

An Investigation

"Are you all right, Mrs. Yardley?" Dr. Street said. "Gloria, would you get Mrs. Yardley some water? And her chair?"

I brought Mrs. Yardley her chair, and Dr. Street helped her into it. I got water, too. While Mrs. Yardley was sipping it, her yardstick up by the blackboard fell down with a clatter, as if it really *had* fainted.

I went back to my seat. Dr. Street pulled up a student desk for herself.

"Mr. Dixon told me there was a problem in

this class about pencils in the ceiling," she said.

"There was," Mrs. Yardley agreed.

"I was wondering who stuck the pencils in the ceiling," Dr. Street said. "Would the person who did it please stand up?"

Julian coughed. Shavaun shuffled his feet.

"You see, looking at it as a scientist, I can see it's a very difficult thing to do," Dr. Street said. "It takes proper launch speed and perfect trajectories. Not everybody would have had the imagination or the skill to do it. So who did it? All of you?"

Dr. Street's eyes were powerful. When she looked at us, we felt like we had to tell. The room was so full of silence I thought it would burst, and then Billy Watkins stood up and said, "I did it."

Mrs. Yardley gasped. "Not you, Billy!" she said.

"I did it," Billy repeated. "I angled them just right. I got it all done in four minutes and

fifteen seconds. I think it must be something for the *Guinness Book of World Records*."

"What you did is a great example of misapplied intelligence," Dr. Street conceded. "It might belong in the *Guinness Book of World Records*. But I heard you said everybody else did it. Why?"

Billy looked embarrassed. He shrugged. "I like to fool people," he said.

"Tell about the coffee, too!" Latisha said. "I bet you did that, too!"

Billy didn't say anything.

"What's this about coffee?" Dr. Street asked.

"Nothing. Nothing much," Billy said.

"Go ahead and *tell*!" Julian said.

"Yeah, go ahead and *tell*!" everybody said.

"What about coffee?" Dr. Street said. She never took her eyes off Billy.

"I took Gloria's bubble gum and stuck it in Mrs. Yardley's coffee. That's all."

"Billy—you didn't!" Mrs. Yardley said.

"And why?" Dr. Street asked.

"I don't know," Billy said. "It made me feel good."

"The rest of you, how do you feel about the things Billy does?"

"Bad," Julian said. "Bad for him and bad for us and just plain bad."

"Angry," Ashok said.

"It makes me want to get even," Latisha said. "Gloria is a nice person. And for just no reason, Billy, you made her suffer."

"He makes us all suffer," Roger Smith said.

"Yeah," everybody said.

"Billy," Dr. Street said, "I have some advice for you. Go find the crazy fearball fireball that's making you do bad things. Because if you don't change, you will have no friends, and the only person you'll be fooling is yourself.

"You students, you be the measure for Billy. You tell him when he's doing bad or doing good. Because by himself, he doesn't know."

"I am sorry," Billy said. "I'm sorry about the pencils and the coffee. I am sorry I called Gloria Onion Head."

"Let's have some applause for Billy," Dr. Street said, "because he's going to change."

So we all applauded Billy, everyone but Mrs. Yardley.

Dr. Street stood up.

"I'm sorry I've got to go," she said. "It's been a pleasure to talk to you all. Thank you, Mrs. Yardley. And Gloria—I'll see you."

There wasn't time to applaud her. We waved.

The Rocket Tree

The rest of that day Mrs. Yardley was very quiet. It seemed as if she didn't know how to treat us. She never even picked her yardstick up off the floor. Julian did that for her.

The next day she told us she had something important to say, and she hoped we would remember it. She said she was sorry for the mistaken judgments she had made. She said she hoped we'd do like Dr. Street said, and study hard and make her proud.

For the rest of the year, she didn't tap the

floor once with her yardstick, or even carry it around, and she said we could sharpen our pencils whenever they needed it. We kind of missed Grinding Time, though. It had been fun.

Billy Watkins stopped trying to trick us. I think he's really changing.

Everybody in our class thought Dr. Street was a hero for getting him to change. And everybody thought I was a hero for actually knowing Dr. Grace Street.

I thought a lot about what Dr. Street said—about daring to do the things you care about—things you're afraid to try.

There was one thing I wanted to do most, something special that scared me. That was climbing Old Rocket.

Old Rocket is an enormous pine tree, the oldest and tallest tree in the park. Julian and I have called it Old Rocket ever since we were little, because of the way its top branches taper to a point. Sometimes from the ground they look almost black, like the burnt tip of a rocket sent into space.

Julian and I always said we would climb it someday, but we never had. It has lots and lots of branches that go out wide and straight, so it wouldn't be so hard. It's just because Old Rocket is so tall that we never dared to try.

Old Rocket stands like a green tower on top of the steepest hill in the park. I went there alone early one Saturday morning. The sun wasn't up when I started climbing the hill. I felt a little scared. I kept wondering if, when I got to the top of the hill, I would just turn around and go home.

Then I got there, and I was amazed—right behind Old Rocket's trunk there was a huge red burning ball of fire! It looked just the way Dr. Street had described a person's energy looking. At first I thought mine had jumped out of me somehow. Then I realized I was

looking at the sunrise. I looked away, because the sun is such a great big ball of energy that it can burn your eyes.

I looked up instead, into the green web of Old Rocket's branches. They almost hid the sky and seemed to have no end.

I touched Old Rocket's trunk and the deep age wrinkles in its bark.

"I'm going to climb you," I told it, "and I never did climb so high, so help me, please."

I felt my fear like a nervous gray sun bouncing around inside me, and Old Rocket's stillness, so big it seemed even bigger than the tree.

Then my hands caught the lowest branch of Old Rocket, and I scrambled up and onto it. I sat there for a minute, looking up, and then I knew I didn't have so much to fear. Even if I fell, Old Rocket had so many branches I wouldn't fall far before it caught me. I wouldn't fall to earth.

A breeze came up and made a sighing in Old

Rocket's high branches. It seemed like a word the tree was saying, gentle as a whisper, mighty as a roar. I couldn't understand the word exactly, but it seemed like Old Rocket's way of telling me to climb.

I started higher. Pine sap got on my clothes, and I had to duck and twist between branches. I couldn't see the ground at all. Through the top of the tree, bits of sky were showing. They made it easier to see the way up.

I stopped thinking about where I'd been and where I was going. When I didn't think about the whole climb, I wasn't scared I couldn't make it. I knew I could always take one more little step. I remembered what Dr. Street had said about big things really being little, and I understood it.

Still my stomach felt all tense, as if it was separate from me, a little animal that was scared. All the way, I tried to reassure it and tell it I would be careful and it was safe.

I got to the highest branches of Old Rocket. There were no more big ones. I was as near the top as anyone could ever go.

I sat on the last thick branch and leaned against the trunk of Old Rocket. I breathed deeply and I dared to look out.

I could see our whole town—my block, the roof of our house, my school and the playground, Main Street with all the stores, and a few tiny people moving around. Everything looked so small, but so clear. It was wonderful to see it. It was amazing.

I sat balanced on my branch. I sat up where Old Rocket made its whispers and its roars, and it seemed it was saying many words, and they were all beautiful. It was saying that someone who could climb Old Rocket could become an astronaut, or a doctor, or anything in the world. It was saying that I could be like Dr. Grace Street, a person who had tamed her fear.

But I didn't want to think too much. I still

had to climb down. When you make little things out of a big thing, it's a mistake to make the little things back into a big thing. Really, I thought, every single thing is both big and little.

I went down slowly, without looking any farther than the next branch my feet could touch. And then suddenly the earth was very close, just a little way below me. I hung from the lowest branch and dropped to the ground.

Looking up, I couldn't see where Old Rocket had made its words. But I had climbed there. I had heard them.

Afterward

Afterward is always the biggest part of life—so of course that's when a lot of things happened.

School got better. Our class concentrated and did really well on the state tests. At the end of the year, Mrs. Yardley told us she was retiring from teaching. She said we were not only her last class ever, we were her best class ever, and it had been a privilege to teach us. We were almost sorry we ever called her the Dragon of Doom.

After vacation started, Julian talked a lot about climbing Old Rocket. He says he's ready to do it, but Huey should climb, too, and Huey isn't ready yet. I say that we can wait. Maybe Latisha and Tyrone and Shavaun will want to climb, too. I keep it to myself that I did it.

I keep it to myself because I know Julian would feel bad if he knew I climbed first. Some things a person shouldn't keep secret, but keeping this secret makes me feel good.

Sometimes I go visit Old Rocket alone. I feel as if it knows me and is glad for what I did. I tell it things I want to do one day, and I listen to the strange beautiful words it makes with the wind.

It's a long time now since I was promoted out of Ms. Morgan's class and had to leave her. I didn't think I'd see her very much again. I'd be going up and up, from grade to grade, and all the time I'd be going further away from her.

But Ms. Morgan, who I never thought would change at all, has changed! Next year, she's going to teach fifth! And she will be my teacher.

I got a postcard from Dr. Street in July. The picture on it was of an enormous blue sea. Out in the middle of all the sparkling blue was a sailboat with tall white sails leaning against the wind. Four people were calling out to each other from the rigging and the deck. They looked very happy and free.

The message side of the postcard read:

Dear Gloria,

How are you? I hope your year with Mrs. Yardley went better. Right now I'm in the Mediterranean, but I was serious when I said I'd be seeing you. I really was very impressed when I met you with how much you want to

learn. I have your phone number, and I'll call you the next time I'm in town. I hope we can have lunch together and get to know each other better.

> *Your friend,*
> *Grace Street*

P.S. Do you still want to be an astronaut? Remember, where you want to be is where you belong.

Another thing happened I almost forgot to mention. My mom was wrong about my onion. It never did rot. It got shrunken and tired-looking, and then, all of a sudden, a bright green shoot sprouted from the top of it. I showed my folks, and they said it was starting to make a whole new onion.

The old onion would be the new onion's food, they said, but it needed more food than that, and I should plant it.

I took it to Julian and Huey's house, and their dad, Mr. Bates, helped us plant it in their garden.

Next winter we'll go to the spot where we planted it. Mr. Bates says the new onion will be full grown then. We'll dig it up gently and clean it off. I can't wait to see it, just like the old one—silky and light tan, glowing like a pearl.

AUTHOR'S NOTE

You can learn more about space and actual astronauts on the internet.

The main NASA site for children has lots of fun activities, photos, and information about space at nasa.gov/kidsclub.

To learn more about individual astronauts and see their photos, go to nasa.gov/astronauts.

NASA offers teachers curriculum support with much information about living in space at nasa.gov/audience/foreducators.

When Gloria's best friend, Julian, tells her
a little fib . . . it turns into a big mess!

Read on for a peek at
this summer adventure!

1.

Why I Tell Stories

I am a nice person. I practically almost always tell the truth. I really don't like making up stories. I only do it when absolutely necessary. That's the way it was at the beginning of the summer.

It was the first morning after school got out. I was sitting in our swing, making circles in the sand with my tennis shoe and watching some ants go by. Every last one was in a hurry.

"Take your time!" I said to them. "This is vacation!"

But they went on running as fast as they

could. They acted like they were all late.

"Where are you going so fast?" I asked.

I wasn't in a hurry. I was happy. My little brother, Huey, was with my dad at his car repair shop. My mother was at her job. I was waiting for my best friend, Gloria. I was thinking how much fun Gloria and I (and Huey, when I let him play with us) would have all summer.

I was thinking so much, I hardly looked at the street. I almost didn't see a girl on a blue bicycle going by fast—and when I did, I thought, "That can't be Gloria!" because Gloria doesn't have a bicycle.

The girl on the blue bicycle didn't stop. She didn't even look at me.

That was a relief. It couldn't be Gloria.

And then the girl came by once more, a little slower. She had braids just like Gloria's, flying flat out behind her in the breeze.

Still she didn't look at me or stop. So I thought to myself, "It *can't* be Gloria."

But I was worried. I said to myself, "What if it *is* Gloria? What if it's Gloria's bike?"

I decided to go into action.

I got out of the swing. I stood with my feet as close together as possible, my hands rolled into fists, and my eyes shut tight.

I kept my eyes shut for a long time, concentrating.

On the blackness inside my eyelids, I pictured the blue bicycle.

Then I made my wish, very slowly, out loud, three times.

"Let it not be Gloria's.

"Let it NOT be Gloria's.

"Let it not be GLORIA'S," I said.

The air, the trees, and the sky were all stamped with my wish.

I opened my eyes.

A face was one inch from my face.

It was Gloria's.

She said, "Did anybody call my name?"

The world came into focus. Behind Gloria, on the grass, I saw a blue bicycle.

I unrolled my fists.

I moved my feet apart.

"Your name?" I said to Gloria.

"Yes, Julian," Gloria said. "My name. Also, I think I should tell you, about thirty thousand ants are crawling up the back of your pants."

I looked behind me. Sure enough, Gloria was right. I moved away from the ant trail and brushed the ants off my pants.

"I thought I heard my name," Gloria said again. "I thought I heard you say something really strange. I thought I heard you say 'Let it not be Gloria's.' "

"Oh, *that,*" I said. "I was making a wish."

"But weren't you saying my name?" Gloria persisted.

I was embarrassed. "Of course not," I said. "Of course I wasn't saying your name."

"What were you saying, then, Julian?" Gloria asked.

It was one of those times when I didn't want to tell the truth. And just like magic, it came to me—what I could make up.

ABOUT THE AUTHOR

Ann Cameron is the bestselling author of the Julian's World series and many other popular books for children. She lives in Guatemala. Find her online at anncameronbooks.com.